# SARAH'S DISAPPOINTMENT

## AN ADVENTIST GIRL STORY

~ BOOK FOUR ~

# JEAN BOONSTRA

**Pacific Press® Publishing Association**
Nampa, Idaho
Oshawa, Ontario, Canada
www.pacificpress.com

Edited by Tim Lale
Designed by Dennis Ferree
Cover illustration by Matthew Archambault


Copyright © 2002 by
Pacific Press® Publishing Association
Printed in United States of America
All Rights Reserved


Additional copies of this book may be purchased at
http://www.adventistbookcenter.com

*Library of Congress Cataloging-in-Publication Data*

Boonstra, Jean Elizabeth.
  Sarah's disappointment : Sarah 1842-1844 / Jean
Elizabeth Boonstra.
      p. cm. — (Adventist girl series; bk. 4)
  Summary: Believing that Jesus' second coming
will occur on October 22, 1844, the Barnes family
and many of their friends prepare for the imminent
event, only to be disappointed until Pastor Robinson
proposes a biblical explanation.
  ISBN 0-8163-1888-3
  [1. Seventh-day Adventists] I. Title.

  PZ7.B64613 Sar 2002
  —dc21                                    2001052348

02 03 04 05 06 • 5 4 3 2 1

# Contents

# Dedication

To my husband, Shawn, for his
constant love and encouragement.
To our daughter, Natalie, whose
birth on October 22, 1999
was a most joyous event.

## CHAPTER 1

# A
# New Dress

*Splash!*

Sarah Barnes dropped a petticoat into the wash water. She picked up a bar of soap and scrubbed. Bubbles jumped and twirled around her hands. Sarah lifted the petticoat out of the soapy water and rinsed it in a bucket of fresh water. She carried the dripping garment to the clothesline and carefully clipped it on.

Sarah reached for the next petticoat and sighed. The summer sun was beating down on the back of her neck. Loose hair escaped from her cotton cap and clung to her forehead. *This is going to take me all day,* she thought. The summer heat made her feel sleepy.

Emily banged open the kitchen door and trotted into the late-morning sunshine. Her bare toes dug into the ground as she raced around the garden. Breathless, she stopped in front of Sarah's washing tub. Missy the cat scampered across the garden. "Sarah," she panted, "will you come and play with me?"

Sarah didn't look up. "I can't," she said, still scrubbing. "I have to wash all of these clothes." She dipped the petticoat into the rinse water and then carried it to the clothesline. *I wish that I were a thousand miles from here,* she thought as she fastened the clothespin.

Splash! Bang!

"Emily!" Sarah yelled. She watched, helpless, as Emily pulled the tub full of water down on top of herself. Sarah grabbed the tub and pulled her little sister up off the ground. "Emily," Sarah asked crossly, "what on earth were you doing?"

Emily coughed and wiped the water from her face. "I was helping you," she said, her big eyes looking sad. "Then you could play with me."

Mrs. Barnes ran out of the kitchen. "Emily!" she called. "Are you all right?" She grabbed Emily's arm and looked her over, up and down.

"She's fine, Mother," Sarah said. "She was trying to help me with the washing." Sarah helped her mother undo Emily's dress. Emily squirmed until the wet, muddy dress fell at her feet. Sarah giggled as Emily picked pieces of wet grass off her bare legs. At least this was more interesting than doing the washing.

"What is all of the noise?" Grammy walked up the path that led from her rooms. She was fastening her bonnet over her neat bun.

"Grammy," Emily bubbled, "I was helping Sarah!"

Grammy did not look pleased. "I see that," she said.

"Go inside the house please, Emily," said Mrs. Barnes. "We'll find a dry dress for you to wear."

Emily scampered through the grass.

"Sarah," Mrs. Barnes said, dropping the muddy dress onto the pile of laundry. "Please go and refill the washing tub." Mrs. Barnes wiped her forehead with the back of her hand. "You'll have to heat more water over the fire."

"Yes, Mother," said Sarah. She wiped the mud off the tub.

"Would you mind helping Emily get changed?" Mrs. Barnes asked Grammy.

Grammy didn't answer right away. "I suppose that I could do that," she finally said.

"Thank you," Mrs. Barnes said.

Carefully, Grammy stepped around the

patch of wet, muddy grass and walked toward the house.

Sarah poured a little of the rinse water over her hands to clean them.

"Come on," Mrs. Barnes said, lifting one end of the washtub. "I'll help you fill this up." Her hazel eyes sparkled in the sunshine. "I'll even help you with the washing if Samuel stays asleep."

"Thank you," Sarah said. It was nice to have her mother to herself for a little while.

They walked to the well and filled the washtub with water. Mrs. Barnes laughed as the cool water sloshed over the edge of the tub and onto her feet. Sarah felt happy.

"The hot water is ready," Sarah called, lifting the pot off the fire.

"All right," said Mrs. Barnes, opening the kitchen door for her. "Carry it outside, and let's start the washing again."

Sarah poured the hot water into the cool water in the tub. She tested the temperature with her pinkie finger. It was just right.

She dropped the bar of soap in and started scrubbing. She scrubbed until the dirt and grass stains lifted off the faded cotton. Sarah handed the soapy dress to her mother.

Mrs. Barnes rinsed it in the fresh water. "Sarah," she said, lifting the dress out and inspecting it. "This is your winter dress, isn't it?"

"Yes," Sarah answered, plopping the next dress into the water.

Mrs. Barnes turned the dress around. "Does it still fit you?" she asked.

"Just barely," said Sarah. "The sleeves are too short and always creep up my arms."

Mrs. Barnes wrung out the dress. "I think that I have a summer project for you," she said, carrying the dripping dress to the clothesline. She grinned as she wiped her hands on her apron. "You are going to sew yourself a new dress."

"Really, Mother?" Sarah exclaimed. "I've never made myself a dress before. What if I don't know what to do?"

# A New Dress

Mrs. Barnes laughed. "Don't worry," she said. "I'll be here to help you."

"Mother," Sarah asked, "when can we get the material? I can't wait."

Mrs. Barnes thought for a moment. "We'll go today," she said. "As soon as we're finished here, we'll get Father to hitch up the horse and buggy. We'll take along a lunch. It will be great fun!"

"Oh, Mother," Sarah said excitedly, "It sounds wonderful."

"Now more scrubbing and less talking," Mrs. Barnes teased. "We have to hurry."

Sarah quickly scrubbed and washed, and daydreamed about her new dress.

* * * * *

Sarah closed her eyes. The warm breeze cooled her face as they rode in the wagon. She snuggled Samuel in close to her. He sighed happily in her arms.

"Mother," Katie hollered from the bench behind them, "Emily pinched me."

"Did not!" Emily quickly called back.

Mrs. Barnes turned and looked sharply over her shoulder. "Girls, please stop fighting. We had a pleasant afternoon in the city, and I don't want it spoiled now."

"Yes, Mother," Katie and Emily said together. Everything was quiet again.

"Thank you for the material, Mother," Sarah said. I can't wait to start on my dress. Do you really think that I can make it all by myself?"

"Of course you can," Mrs. Barnes said, laughing. "It will just take some thoughtful effort and a lot of patience. One day soon you may have to sew dresses for your own family."

Sarah blushed. "Not all that soon," she said.

Mrs. Barnes patted her on the knee. "You are growing up to be a very gracious young lady," she said. "I'm proud of you."

# A New Dress

"Thank you," Sarah said. She ran her hand over the pile of smooth, satiny material sitting on the bench beside her. *I'm going to make the most beautiful dress in the world*, she thought. *I'm going to make Mother very proud.*

Mrs. Barnes drew in the reins. The horses slowed to a trot. "Look, girls. Your father is at the Wigginses' farm."

Mrs. Barnes pulled the horses to a stop. Mr. Wiggins and Mr. Barnes were leaning against the fence talking, while Mrs. Wiggins was pulling clean, dry clothes from the clothesline.

"Hello, neighbors," said Mr. Wiggins with a big friendly smile. He took off his hat and rested it in his enormous hand.

Sarah smiled at him.

"Let me have a look at that baby boy of yours," he said, admiring baby Samuel.

"Isn't he gorgeous?" Sarah said.

"He surely is," said Mr. Wiggins, beaming. "That is a fine son you have, Edward." He laughed and slapped Mr. Barnes on the back. "Almost as good looking as my littlest grandson."

Mrs. Wiggins poked her head over the side of the wagon. She smiled down at Samuel. Her blue-gray eyes nearly matched her hair. "Fred, you know that our grandson is a terror!" she said. "This little boy will be an angel!"

Mr. Wiggins laughed. "She's right!"

"Beautiful color," Mrs. Wiggins said, noticing Sarah's material. "Are you making a new dress, Margaret?"

"Sarah is making herself a dress," said Mrs. Barnes proudly.

Mrs. Wiggins looked impressed. "Very nice," she said, running her hand over the soft green-gray fabric.

Mr. Wiggins and Mr. Barnes leaned their backs against the wagon. They talked while Mrs. Barnes and Mrs. Wiggins discussed ideas for Sarah's dress.

"Do you still believe that the world is coming to an end?" Sarah heard Mr.

Wiggins ask her father. Sarah listened carefully. She wondered what her father would say. Lately, the Barnes family had not talked about the end of the world very much. It had been many months since they thought that Jesus would return. Sarah felt as though life was returning to the way it had been before. She liked that. She was happy.

"I do," Mr. Barnes answered. "I still believe the Bible prophecies, and they all indicate that something significant will happen this year. I still trust in our Lord. He is a loving, faithful God who has never let us down."

Sarah frowned. She felt angry inside. She was angry with her father and with herself too. She knew that what he had said was true, but she didn't want to believe it. She listened.

"I admire your faith," Mr. Wiggins said. He patted Mr. Barnes on the arm.

Mr. Barnes smiled. "God bless you," he answered.

Mrs. Wiggins put Sarah's material down beside her.

"Mother," piped up little Emily from the bench behind them, "I'm hungry."

Everyone laughed.

"Enough talking, you two," Mrs. Wiggins said to her husband and Mr. Barnes. "A little girl is hungry. Come on inside now, Fred!"

Mr. Wiggins chuckled and waved goodbye.

"Goodbye," they called. Mr. Barnes hopped up into the wagon and took the reins. Mrs. Barnes slid over next to Sarah.

"Good news," said Mr. Barnes, snapping the reins. The horses trotted toward home. "There is going to be a camp meeting in Exeter in a few weeks. Mr. Wiggins has agreed to watch the farm. Who would like to go?"

Katie fairly bounced off the bench. "Oh, Father," she cried, "I love camp meeting. I want to go! I'll tell Mr. Wiggins exactly how to take care of Pepper."

# A New Dress

"I'm sure that Mr. Wiggins knows how to take care of a cow," Mr. Barnes said with a laugh.

"Pepper is special," Katie said, poking her head in between her mother and father.

"You're right," Mr. Barnes said. "I'm sorry."

Katie seemed happy with his answer and bounced back to her seat.

"Camp meeting would be a nice change of pace," said Mrs. Barnes. "Emily will adore playing with all of the other children her age. We should go."

Mr. Barnes pulled the wagon into the yard and up to the front door. "It's settled then," he said. "The Barneses are going to camp meeting."

"Yea," yelled Katie, jumping out of the wagon, her ponytails bobbing behind her.

Sarah sat in her seat and scowled. No one had asked her, and she did not want to go to camp meeting. Absolutely, definitely not.

## CHAPTER 2

# Camp Meeting in Exeter

"Glory to God! Glory to God!" a voice shouted.

"Come on, Pam," said Sarah, quickly walking past the white peaked tent.

Pam slowed down and poked her blond head through the door.

Sarah crossed her arms and groaned.

In spite of all of her protests throughout the week, Sarah was now at camp meeting in Exeter, New Hampshire. She was not happy about it.

# SARAH'S DISAPPOINTMENT

"Glory to God! Glory to God!" The shouting and clapping rang out from the tent.

"Come on, Pam," Sarah called again. "Let's go."

Pam waved Sarah over. "Come and look," she whispered.

Sarah sighed and stomped over to look through the door of the tent. All through the day before and all through the night, the people inside, all of them from Watertown, Massachusetts, had been shouting and clapping. It was annoying to Sarah. She poked her head around past Pam and looked inside. Men and women were dancing and clapping and shouting, "Glory to God! Glory to God!"

"Have you ever seen anything like it?" Pam whispered. "Father told me that they are trying to say 'Glory to God!' nine hundred and ninety-nine times in a row."

Sarah shook her head. "Crazy," she whispered. "We'd better go, before someone notices us."

"You're right," Pam said.

Sarah and Pam walked along the dusty path. Ladies in long sweeping gowns and men in suits and top hats hurried past them. They were all going to the opening in the trees called The Stand for the evening meeting.

"I have a good idea," Sarah said brightly.

Pam looked up at her friend suspiciously. "What?" she asked.

Sarah's brown eyes twinkled. She looked around to make sure that no one was listening and then whispered in Pam's ear. "Let's not go to the meeting. Let's sneak down to the creek and wade in the water."

"Sarah!" Pam cried. "We'll be caught for sure. Our mothers are waiting for us."

"Shh," Sarah scolded. "Someone will hear you." She tucked a stray hair behind her ear and looked around. "We can say that we couldn't find them, and so we sat at the back. We've heard these sermons a hundred times before. We can pretend we were there."

Pam didn't say anything for a moment. A woman carrying a baby brushed past them. "It is awfully hot," Pam finally said.

Sarah's face lit up. "You won't regret this," she said happily. "It will be the most fun we've had since we got here." She grabbed Pam's arm. "Let's cut through the trees right over there," she said, pointing to her right. "Someone might see us if we take the trail."

Pam giggled nervously.

"Sarah! Pam! Wait for me!"

Sarah's heart sank. She couldn't believe her ears. "It's Katie," she whispered quickly to Pam. "Let's just keep walking and pretend that we didn't hear her."

Sarah and Pam walked as quickly as they could, but Katie soon caught up with them. "Hi," she said breathlessly.

Sarah felt very annoyed. "What do you want, Katie?" she asked.

Katie skipped along to keep up with her older sister and Pam. "Nothing," she answered, her smile disappearing. "Just to walk with you to the meeting."

"We'll meet you there," Sarah said.

"Can't I walk with you?" Katie asked.

"No," Sarah answered coldly. She was in no mood for Katie right now. She just wanted to go to the creek and cool her feet.

"Fine," Katie whined. "I'm going to tell Mother that I saw you and that you wouldn't let me walk with you."

"No, you aren't," Sarah yelled, looking down at her sister with the meanest face she had.

Katie started to cry.

"Sarah," Pam whispered, "she could come with us."

Sarah twirled around, her back to her sister. "No," she blurted out. "I don't want her to."

"Please let me come," Katie sobbed. "I promise that I won't tell."

Pam felt uncomfortable as she looked from Sarah to Katie.

A plump lady slowed as she passed. "Is everything all right here, girls?" she asked, looking concerned.

Sarah smiled brightly. "Just fine," she answered. "We were just helping my little sister inside. Everything is fine." Sarah put her arm around Katie's shoulder. "Come along now, Katie," she said cheerfully.

The plump woman looked at them suspiciously. "All right, then," she said. "Go and find your mothers."

Sarah, Katie, and Pam followed the woman to the stand. "I guess we'd better go listen to the sermon," Sarah whispered to Pam.

"It's probably for the best anyway," Pam whispered back.

Sarah looked for her mother and Mrs. Van Dyke in the sea of people. At last she spotted them. The three girls sat down on the rough wooden bench just as the service began.

After the opening hymn, a man stood to introduce the speaker for the evening. "Brother Joseph Bates, a retired sea captain, will be opening God's Word for us tonight," he said.

Mrs. Barnes leaned over and whispered in Sarah's ear. "Grandfather knew Captain Bates well," she said. "They often discussed the nearness of the Second Advent together."

Sarah smiled, because it was nice to be reminded of Grandfather. She settled into her seat and watched Captain Bates as he opened his Bible. She listened carefully for a little while, but it was hard to concentrate. She had heard the same kind of sermon so many times over the past two years. The warm summer air made her feel sleepy. Sarah blinked her eyes to keep them open.

"It is too late, brother!"

# SARAH'S DISAPPOINTMENT

Sarah watched, amazed, as a woman sitting a few rows in front of her stood to her feet in the middle of Captain Bates's sermon. She raised her hands over her head to get his attention. "It is too late to spend our time upon these truths, with which we are familiar, and which have blessed us in the past. They have served their purpose and their time."

A gasp spread across the crowd. This was very unusual. Captain Bates stood with his mouth open, his Bible open in his hand.

The woman continued. "Brother Samuel Snow has a new message for today. We will all be blessed by its hearing." Just as suddenly as she had stood up, she sat down again.

Sarah was very much awake now.

Captain Bates closed his Bible and thoughtfully took off his spectacles. "Is Brother Snow with us this evening?" he asked.

Heads turned in every direction to look for Mr. Snow. At last, hesitatingly, a slim, dark-haired man stood to his feet. He looked down humbly at the ground.

Captain Bates stood tall and said, "Please, brother. Come and open God's Word and share this message with His faithful ones."

Mr. Samuel Snow walked to the platform and stood behind the pulpit. It was perfectly silent. Not even a cough or a baby's whimper was heard. "Thank you, Brother Bates," he began. "This is most unprecedented."

Mr. Snow opened his Bible that warm August evening and shared a powerful message. Sarah was captivated. She did not understand a lot of what he said. What she did understand was that in the Old Testament God had made many special feast days for the people of Israel. When Jesus came to earth the first time, He fulfilled many of these feasts exactly as the Bible prophets predicted. Mr. Snow explained that Jesus would do the same when He came again the second time.

Sarah sat on the edge of her seat as Mr. Snow flipped the pages in his Bible. He read many Bible texts. "The tenth day of the seventh month is the Jewish Day of Atonement," he preached. "I believe that Jesus will return on this day."

A murmur rippled through the congregation, and was quickly followed by silence. Sarah held her breath.

Mr. Snow looked into the expectant faces of the people gathered before him. "Jesus will return on October 22, 1844."

Sarah forgot that she was not alone. "Oh!" she said out loud. The sound of her own voice startled her, and she quickly looked around, embarrassed. No one seemed to notice, though. They were all as mesmerized as she was.

The meeting ended very differently from the way it had begun. Without saying anything, Mrs. Barnes handed sleeping baby Samuel to Sarah. Sarah tucked him into her arms. Mrs. Barnes picked up Emily. Katie and Sarah followed them down the aisle and out toward the path.

The sun was just setting as Sarah walked along the dusty path to their tent. A soft orange glow hung in the summer air. Gently, Sarah laid Samuel down on the little bed Mrs. Barnes had made for him. He squirmed a little, and seemed to smile in his sleep.

Sarah quickly changed into her nightgown. She brushed her hair and kneeled to say her prayers. *Thank You, Jesus,* she prayed. *Thank You for making me come to camp meeting.* Sarah lifted her patchwork quilt and crawled under it. Katie scampered across the bed and crawled in beside her.

"Good night, girls," Mrs. Barnes said, leaning over them to kiss them good night. "Sleep well."

"Good night," Sarah and Katie answered.

Sarah lay still in the little bed made out of quilts. She looked up at the top of the tent. "Sorry that I was mean to you, Katie," she whispered.

Katie opened her eyes. "It's all right," she said sleepily, "I already forgave you."

Sarah smiled to herself. Darkness settled over the tent. The sheet around their sleeping area lifted, and Mr. Barnes stepped in.

"Shh," Sarah heard her mother whisper, "don't wake the children."

Sarah listened as her father and mother talked softly. As she rolled over, Sarah realized that she could no longer hear shouting and clapping coming from the Watertown tent. A peaceful quiet hung over the camp. It was as if they had all been thirsty for Mr. Snow's message and were now satisfied.

CHAPTER 3

# Miss Button's Announcement

Sarah dipped her quill pen into the inkwell in front of her. Carefully she placed it on the page in her copybook and wrote out her last arithmetic problem—four thousand three hundred fifty-six plus one thousand eight hundred ninety-seven. Sarah scrunched up her nose. She added the seven and the six and carried the one. In a moment she had the correct answer—six thousand two hundred fifty-three. Sarah smiled. She was very good at arithmetic and enjoyed it. She laid her pen beside her copybook. She was finished for the day.

Sarah wiggled the kinks out of her fingers. She could hear the sound of pens scratching on paper all around her. Alannah looked up at her, frustrated.

"Are you finished already?" she whispered, her eyebrows furrowed.

"Of course," said Sarah with a wink.

Alannah scowled and dipped her pen again.

Sarah reached under her seat and picked up her stitching sampler. She pulled a piece of light-blue thread through the fabric. She was almost finished with the checkered border. When it was done, her sampler would be completed. As she stitched, Sarah dreamed about her new dress. She imagined the soft satin material flowing in pleats over her petticoats. She had only cut out the material so far. She was eager to begin the sewing.

# Miss Button's Announcement

"May I have your attention please, class," said Miss Button, Sarah's teacher.

Sarah put down her sampler.

Miss Button stood in front of her desk. She rubbed a blotch of ink off her right hand. "That is all the time we have for today," she announced. "We are ending our lesson a little earlier than usual."

A chorus of happy whispers rose up from the students. Miss Button did not try to quiet them as she usually did. Instead she listened to them thoughtfully.

"I have an announcement," she said, placing the ink-stained rag on the desk. Miss Button's young face was bright, but her eyes looked tired. "As many of you know," Miss Button continued, "I believe that our Lord, Jesus Christ, will return to this earth soon. In fact, I believe that He will return by October 22, which is less than a month away." She looked around the room at each student's face. "It is because I believe that He is returning so very soon that I have decided to resign as your teacher. I want to devote my full energy to telling people about the soon end of the world."

Sarah gasped. She knew that Miss Button believed in the soon return of Jesus, but she did not expect this.

"School will be cancelled until a replacement teacher may be found." Miss Button slowly walked behind her desk and picked up her neat stack of books. She held her head high. "Good afternoon, children. May God bless you all." Miss Button blinked hard, but a tear escaped and ran down her cheek. Quickly she walked down the aisle and to the door.

Sarah gathered her books into a little pile and placed her sampler on top of them. She reached under her chair for her lunch pail. It didn't seem real. She couldn't believe that this was the last day of school. Ever.

"Goodness," Alannah whispered. She closed her copybook. "Wait until I tell

# Miss Button's Announcement

Mamó and Daideó. They will be so surprised."

"I just can't believe it," Sarah whispered back. She gathered her belongings and walked past the hearth and toward the door.

Sarah curtsied politely. "Goodbye, Miss Button," she said.

Miss Button smiled down at her. "God bless you, Miss Barnes."

Sarah couldn't help herself. She reached out and hugged her teacher.

Miss Button seemed surprised! "Don't worry," she whispered, hugging her back. "If we don't see each other on this earth again, then we will certainly see each other in heaven."

Sarah wiped a tear from her cheek. "I pray so," she said. "Thank you."

Miss Button winked and squeezed her hand.

Sarah walked down the wooden steps that had become so familiar over the last few years. She sat in the cool shade of the maple tree and looked back at the little red schoolhouse. *I'll miss you*, she said quietly.

Pam and Alannah walked toward her, hair blowing in the breeze. "This feels strange," Pam said, sitting down beside her. "The last day of school, maybe forever."

"I feel like I'm dreaming," said Sarah.

"I feel a little funny," Alannah said, crinkling her freckled nose. "I don't believe that the world is coming to an end, but what if it is?"

"It isn't," Nickie Cooper blurted out loudly. She tromped past them, her arms full of books.

Sarah rolled her eyes.

"They have vivid imaginations," Nickie said abruptly. "I've tried telling you, Alannah, that these Millerites are crazy." She glared at Sarah and Pam. "Now our school has been closed. My father will not be happy about this." Nickie's face was red with anger.

Alannah sighed and shrugged her shoulders. She had learned that arguing with Nickie was useless. "All right, Nickie," she said, standing up. "You can believe whatever you want, but so can Sarah and Pam."

Nickie started to say something, but instead she twirled around as Peter and David walked by.

"David!" Nickie cried.

David Cooper looked over his shoulder at his sister. "Yes, Nickie," he said meekly.

Nickie plopped her stack of books on top of his. "Carry my books home for me," she demanded. "My arms are tired."

"But," David protested. "I have my own books."

"I don't care," Nickie replied, wiping dust off the front of her dress. "I'm going home to tell father what happened. Come along, David."

David shifted the heavy stack of books. "I'll be there in a little while," he answered.

Nickie smirked and marched across the field.

"Let me help you with those books, Dave," Peter said, grabbing a handful. He piled the books into his strong arms.

"Thanks," said David, relieved. He pushed up his spectacles with his free hand. David shuffled his feet and looked up shyly. "May I talk to you about something?" he stammered.

"Sure, my friend," Peter said.

David smiled awkwardly and looked down at the ground. "Not with Alannah," he said. He didn't look up.

Alannah's cheeks turned as red as her hair. She stood up and picked up her books. "All right," she said. "I guess I'll go home now."

Sarah felt sorry for her. "Come over to my house on Sunday, Alannah," she said cheerfully.

"I think so," said Alannah. "Well, 'bye then."

There was an uncomfortable silence as the little group watched Alannah walk across the field.

Pam spoke first. "What is it, David?" she asked.

David wiped a bead of sweat off his forehead. "I've been studying the Bible," he said hesitantly. He looked into each of their faces. "I remember the sermon that Mr. Miller preached a few years ago," he said. "I've tried many times to find something wrong with what he preached. I cannot. I believe, now, like you do that Jesus will return on October 22 of this year."

Tears welled up in Sarah's eyes. All this time, David had been studying the Second Advent message and had never told them.

Peter slapped him on the shoulder. "God bless you," he said, his voice full of

43

emotion. "Only you would remember a sermon from two years ago!"

Everyone laughed.

"Have you told anyone else?" Sarah asked seriously.

"I told Father last night," said David. "He told me that I must forget about all of this foolishness, or he will disown me as a son." David's face changed. He looked stronger than Sarah had ever seen him look before. "I told him that I would do no such thing."

"Good for you, David," Pam said. "We are your friends, and we are here for you."

"Let's pray together," Sarah said.

The little group knelt that day under the maple tree, and they prayed for each other. It was not what usually happened in the schoolyard, but this was an unusual time.

"Amen," Peter said, the last one to pray.

Sarah pushed herself up onto her feet. She felt shy all of a sudden.

# Miss Button's Announcement

David struggled to lift up his stack of books. "Thanks," he mumbled, without looking up. Sarah and Pam and Peter watched him stumble across the field toward home. They stood in silence for what seemed like a long time. No one seemed to know what to say. The moment was too magical.

## CHAPTER 4

# A Day
## in
# Portsmouth

Sarah spooned some porridge into her bowl. She nibbled a little from the end of her spoon and then put it down. Her stomach felt full of butterflies. She felt excited and scared all at once. Today was October 21. It was the last day before the end of the world!

Mr. Barnes pushed his empty bowl toward the center of the table and folded his copy of *The New Hampshire Gazette* in half. He lifted it up to show his wife. "Margaret," he said, "we made the front page again."

# SARAH'S DISAPPOINTMENT

"Let me see, Father," said Katie excitedly.

"Please don't interrupt, Katie," Mrs. Barnes said, rocking Samuel in her arms. "I've seen it," she said to Mr. Barnes. "You may show the girls."

"Thank you, Mother," Katie said, pushing herself up onto her knees, almost knocking over her bowl.

Mr. Barnes placed the newspaper on the table between Sarah and Katie. Emily hopped out of her chair and pushed her face up to the table's edge. She didn't want to miss anything.

The newspaper headline read, "The End of the World Man." Sarah read the first few lines. *William Miller and his many followers believe that the world will soon come to an end. The Millerites believe that Jesus Christ will return to earth tomorrow. On October 22.*

Sarah looked up from the paper. "There have been articles in the paper about Mr. Miller every day," she said.

# A Day in Portsmouth

"Yes, there have," Mr. Barnes answered. "I have read more about Mr. Miller than I have about our next president the last few weeks." Mr. Barnes lifted up the newspaper and looked at it thoughtfully. "Our message is known around the world. Many anticipate Jesus' return tomorrow." His forehead furrowed with concern. "I am going into the city to hand out pamphlets, if that is all right with you, Margaret."

Mrs. Barnes smiled. "Yes, Edward. We'll be fine here. You must be about the Lord's work."

Mr. Barnes kissed his wife on the forehead.

"Oh, please, Father," Sarah begged, running her words together all at once. "May I come with you? I won't complain about getting tired or cold or hungry or anything. I promise." Sarah's big brown eyes looked up at her father expectantly.

Mr. Barnes and Mrs. Barnes's eyes met for a moment. Mrs. Barnes nodded. "All right, Sarah," Mr. Barnes answered. "Go and put on a warmer dress, though. It is starting to get cold outside."

"Thank you," Sarah said, pushing her chair out from under the table. She carried her bowl into the kitchen. She overheard Katie complaining, so she moved quickly before her father might change his mind.

"I want to go too," Katie was saying with a pout. Her arms were crossed and her legs dangling off the chair.

Sarah dashed past them and toward the stairs.

"I need your help here today. Who will milk Pepper for me?" Mrs. Barnes asked Katie.

Sarah closed the bedroom door. She put on an extra petticoat and pulled her winter dress over her head. She struggled to get each of the fussy little buttons through their holes. The heavy navy-blue fabric was faded and worn. Sarah frowned and pulled a bonnet down over her ears. Finally she dashed back down the stairs.

# A Day in Portsmouth

"Have fun," said Mrs. Barnes. "Stay close to your father, and listen to what he says."

"Yes, Mother," said Sarah, waving. " 'Bye."

The crisp morning air felt refreshing. Sarah hopped up onto the wagon next to her father. He snapped the reins, and the horses trotted down the road. Sarah was excited. She tried to imagine what the day would be like.

"Whoa," said Mr. Barnes, pulling back on the reins as they approached the Wigginses' farm. Mr. Wiggins was carrying a small box, he placed it in the back of his wagon.

"Mr. Wiggins," called Mr. Barnes. "Good morning to you."

Mr. Wiggins waved. "Good morning," he called and lumbered toward them. "I'm ready for the end," he said, lifting his hat and wiping the sweat from his forehead. "We've given away all of our earthly possessions."

"Everything?" Mr. Barnes asked, surprised.

Mr. Wiggins smiled. "Yes," he said happily. "We wait joyfully for the return of Jesus tomorrow. What a blessed event it will be! I can't believe that I didn't accept this truth sooner. Thank you for sharing it with me, Edward." He reached into his pocket and pulled out a small envelope. "I almost forgot," he said quietly, placing the envelope in Mr. Barnes's hand. "I owe you this."

"But—" Mr. Barnes began to speak.

"Please," Mr. Wiggins interrupted. "I want to finish things on this earth properly."

Mr. Barnes placed the envelope of money in his pocket. "Thank you," he said.

"We are going into the city to wait for Jesus' return with our daughter and her husband and our grandson." Mr. Wiggins shook Mr. Barnes's hand. "God bless you until we meet again on the other side."

"Yes," said Mr. Barnes. "God bless you."

Mr. Wiggins waved as they moved away along the road.

"Father?" Sarah asked quietly. She almost didn't want to disrupt him. He seemed to be deep in thought.

"Yes, Sarah," Mr. Barnes answered.

"Did Mr. and Mrs. Wiggins give away everything?" she asked.

"It appears so," Mr. Barnes answered. "Some people would say that they are crazy. I think that they have great faith."

Sarah pulled a blanket over her legs and watched the countryside pass by. She thought about Mr. and Mrs. Wiggins and about the next day. *I wonder if I will be afraid,* she thought. The horses pulled the wagon steadily along. They drove along Court Street, past the beautiful white-stone courthouse with its carved wreaths. Mr. Barnes guided the horses to the left and down Pleasant Street. He pulled the wagon to a stop next to the big church called North

Church, just at the entrance to Market Square.

Mr. Barnes hitched the horses. He took a stack of *The Signs of the Times* papers out of the back of the wagon. "Now, keep one eye on me, and don't wander too far away," he said very seriously. "If we get separated you come back here. Look for North Church. That will guide you back to the wagon."

"Yes, Father," Sarah answered, and she followed him down the busy street.

Market Square was full of rushing people. Sarah took a deep breath. She loved the city. She loved watching the people and listening to the door bells jingle as they went in and out of the shops.

Important looking gentlemen in dark suits and women in tall, feathery hats walked past them. Mr. Barnes held a paper out to each one of them. Some of the people graciously accepted it but many walked by Mr. Barnes without even looking at him.

# A Day in Portsmouth

"Get your hats! Free hats!" someone yelled up ahead. "The world is coming to an end tomorrow, and I'm giving away all of my hats!"

A nicely dressed young man quickly brushed past Sarah and trotted up the street. Sarah darted after him.

"Get your hats! Free hats!" The voice was louder now.

Sarah spotted the young man again. He was standing at the edge of a crowd gathered outside a small shop. He pushed his way into the crowd. Sarah followed and was caught up in a sea of people. Men and women were yelling with their arms up in the air. "Over here! I want one!" they called.

*I want to get out of here,* Sarah thought, wishing she hadn't followed the young man into the crowd. *This is terrible. I can't breathe!*

"My last hat!" the voice called again.

Suddenly the shouting stopped, and the crowd of people moved away. Sarah took a deep breath. The young man she had followed placed a new hat on his head and turned and walked away. Sarah stood alone in front of the hat shop. The tired-looking shopkeeper lifted up several empty hat stands. "Run along, little girl," he said, looking at Sarah. "The hats are all gone."

"Yes, sir," she answered, and turned to look for her father. She looked back up the street to where she had last seen him, but he wasn't there anymore. Sarah's heart beat quickly. She looked around her in every direction. She couldn't see her father anywhere. She walked back along the dusty street, peering into the face of each man she passed. None were her father. Hot tears burned her eyes. Sarah sniffled. *I mustn't cry! No, I mustn't!* she told herself. She looked up at the spire on North Church. With tears in her eyes she walked toward it.

"Sarah!"

It was her father. With a desperate look Sarah turned around. "Father!" she called, and then she saw him. He was standing in the doorway of a blacksmith's shop, waving. Sarah ran and embraced him.

"You ran off, didn't you?" Mr. Barnes asked. "Your curiosity got the better of you."

Sarah sniffled again. "Yes, Father," she answered, the tears freely rolling down her cheeks. "I won't do it again."

Mr. Barnes wiped her tears away with his thumb. "I believe you," he said. "You seem to have learned your lesson. Let's keep walking."

Sarah dried her eyes and followed closely behind her father. From then on she wouldn't let him out of her sight.

*Bang. Bang.* A shopkeeper began to nail a long wooden board across his shop window. The man took out several more boards and hammered them to the outside of his store. He covered up the window and door. Sarah watched as he lifted a sign and nailed it to the boards. As he pulled his arm away, Sarah read the sign. "Closed for the soon return of Our Lord, Jesus Christ."

"Father," Sarah said, pulling Mr. Barnes's arm.

Mr. Barnes handed a *Signs* paper to a woman. "Yes," he said over his shoulder.

"That man just nailed boards over his shop window and door because Jesus is coming again tomorrow," she said, pointing behind her.

Mr. Barnes smiled. "Yes," he said, looking toward the shop. "You will see many shops like that today."

Sarah and Mr. Barnes walked up and down the streets of Portsmouth until late in the afternoon. As Mr. Barnes had promised, Sarah saw many boarded-up shops. There were also several shops with newspapers pasted in the windows. The newspapers showed advertisements that the shopkeepers had placed in them. The advertisements said that the shopkeeper was sorry for anything bad they had done to their customers. The shopkeepers wanted to make everything right, just in case the world did come to an end the next day. Still other shopkeepers worked as though tomorrow would just be an ordinary day.

Wearily, Sarah walked beside her father. She didn't dare complain. She had promised him that she wouldn't.

Mr. Barnes handed a paper to a gray-haired woman carrying a stack of neatly folded cloth. "That was my last paper," Mr. Barnes said, putting his hands in his pockets. "I think that it is time to go home now."

"All right, Father," Sarah said. Her feet were sore, and she couldn't wait to sit down. They turned down Daniel Street. Sarah was relieved when they found the wagon. Eagerly she climbed in. It felt wonderful to rest her feet.

Streaks of orange lit up the evening sky as they rode home. As they left the city, the smell of ripe pumpkins and corn filled the air. Mr. Barnes pulled the reins to the left, and the horses turned down their road. They rode past the Wigginses' farm. The farmhouse stood empty and dark against the big New Hampshire sky. *The house looks lonely,* Sarah thought sadly.

In the fields the corn stood tall and majestic. It seemed to go on as far as Sarah could see. *I almost can't believe that this will all be gone tomorrow,* she thought. It still seemed so strange. The peak of their house rose up past the corn stalks. A soft light glowed from the window. It looked warm and friendly, tucked in next to the apple trees. Suddenly Sarah wanted to run inside the house and climb into her mother's lap. She knew that it was silly, and that she was a young lady now, and not a child. Still, she wanted to feel her mother's arms around her, and never, ever leave.

The horses slowed to a stop. "Thank you, Father," Sarah said, stepping out of the wagon, "for letting me come with you today."

# A Day in Portsmouth

Mr. Barnes tied up the horses. "Thank you for your company," he said with a wink. His face looked tired.

Sarah pushed open the door. The smell of hot apple cider floated through the air. "It smells delicious," she said, sniffing the air.

"Welcome back," said Mrs. Barnes. She lifted Emily from her knee and placed her on the floor with her rag doll. She gave Sarah a big hug.

Sarah squeezed her mother tight. It felt good to be home.

"I saved you some soup," Mrs. Barnes said, reaching for her husband's coat. She hung it up for him.

"Thank you, dear," Mr. Barnes said, kissing her cheek. "I will fast tonight, though, so that my mind is clear for tomorrow."

"All right," Mrs. Barnes said with a smile. "Sarah?"

Sarah's stomach rumbled. She felt very hungry. But she wanted to be brave like her father. "No, thank you, Mother," she answered. "I'll fast too."

"Come and sit by the fire and warm up, then," said Mrs. Barnes.

Katie sat up and moved over to one corner of the sofa. "Was it fun?" she asked, curling her feet up underneath her.

"It was," Sarah whispered. "Later I'll tell you what I saw."

Katie smiled. Sarah was glad that she wasn't jealous.

Mrs. Barnes poured a mug of hot apple cider for Sarah. Sarah sipped it slowly.

"Mr. Van Dyke stopped by," Mrs. Barnes said. "I invited the family to spend the day with us tomorrow."

"That will be a blessing," said Mr. Barnes.

"Would you like some apple cider?" Mrs. Barnes asked.

"Yes, please," said Mr. Barnes, warming his hands over the fire.

Katie yawned.

# A Day in Portsmouth

"It sounds like someone is tired," said Mr. Barnes, setting his mug on the table. "Let's have a season of prayer, and then you girls can get some rest. Tomorrow is going to be a big day. We need to especially remember Mr. Miller and his family. They are together on their farm in Low Hampton, New York. Mr. Miller's health is very poor."

The Barnes family knelt together in front of the hearth. They joined hands, all except baby Samuel, who was sleeping peacefully in his cradle next to them. Mr. Barnes, and then Mrs. Barnes, prayed fervently for family, friends, and for Mr. Miller. Sarah, Katie, and Emily each offered their prayers as well. It was a special quiet time. Sarah felt very close to God. She didn't feel afraid.

Mr. Barnes's apple cider turned cold. He had long forgotten about it.

CHAPTER 5

# October 22, 1844

Sarah blinked her eyes. She rolled over onto her elbow and looked around the room. Everything was just as she had left it the night before. Her hairbrush still sat on top of her dresser. Her slippers still lay on the floor beside the bed.

The morning sunlight streamed through the window and spilled onto her quilt. Sarah reached for her treasured doll, Henrietta, and hugged her close. "We're still here," she whispered. "The world hasn't come to an end. At least not yet, anyway."

Sarah put her feet into her slippers and tiptoed over to the window. She pushed aside the cotton curtain and opened it a crack. Katie moaned and pulled her blankets up over her head. Missy yawned. The fresh breeze softly rocked the curtain. Outside everything looked just as it had every other October morning. It didn't feel like the day that the world would come to an end.

Quietly, Sarah poured some water into the wash basin and washed her face. She opened the closet and pulled out a clean petticoat. Her hand brushed against the smooth satin of her partly finished new dress. She reached inside and lifted it out. The soft green satin bodice was finished, but the skirt was still only pinned onto it. Sarah carried the dress over to the mirror and held it up against herself. She imagined the full sleeves and the wide smooth collar that were supposed to be on it. *You would have been a magnificent dress*, she thought with a sigh. Sadly, she hung it back in the closet.

Sarah slipped out of her nightgown and into her old winter dress. She pulled at the tight bodice and too-short sleeves. Her dress was very uncomfortable but Sarah didn't have a choice but to wear it. She brushed her hair and slipped down the stairs.

"Good morning," Mrs. Barnes said. She wiped the dining table with a cloth.

"Good morning," Sarah said with a yawn.

"Would you like something to eat?" Mrs. Barnes asked. "Emily just had some porridge."

Sarah was so hungry that she felt sick. "Is Father still fasting?" she asked.

Mrs. Barnes nodded. "That doesn't mean you have to, though."

"I will," said Sarah. She lifted Emily's rag doll off the floor and set it on the chair.

"Where is Father?" Sarah looked around anxiously.

"He went to go milk Pepper," said Mrs. Barnes, carrying the cloth to the kitchen. "Katie is still asleep."

Sarah's stomach ached. She felt panicky. "Will Father be back soon?" she asked, following her mother into the kitchen.

"Yes, love," said Mrs. Barnes, her hazel eyes full of love. She hugged Sarah against her. "He wouldn't leave us on a day like today," she whispered reassuringly.

The kitchen door creaked open, and Sarah looked up expectantly. Instead of Mr. Barnes, it was Grammy.

"Good morning," said Grammy. "Have the guests arrived yet?" She took off her gloves and set them on the table. She wore her best dress. Sarah adored it. It was emerald green velvet and swept the floor as she walked. The bodice was covered in lace and ribbons. Grammy's black and silver hair glimmered.

# October 22, 1844

Mrs. Barnes squeezed Sarah's shoulder. "They should be here any time," she answered Grammy. "Why don't you make yourself comfortable in the parlor." Mrs. Barnes lifted her apron up over her head and hung it on a nail next to the door. "I'm going upstairs to get dressed. Sarah, will you please watch your brother? He is in the cradle, sleeping."

"Yes, Mother," Sarah answered.

"Margaret! Girls!" Mr. Barnes called, opening the kitchen door. "A wagon just turned down our road. Are you ready?"

Mrs. Barnes flew up the stairs. "I will be in a minute," she called. She knocked on Sarah and Katie's door. "Katie! Get up. Our guests are here." Missy flew out of the room and down the stairs. The cat had been acting a little strange the last few days. Somehow it knew that things were different.

Mr. Barnes carried a pail of milk into the kitchen. He winked at Sarah. "We can always count on your mother running late," he whispered.

Sarah giggled. She lifted Samuel out of the cradle, being careful not to wake him. She gently rocked him for a few moments. Holding him tight, Sarah opened the front door and stepped into the October sunshine. The Van Dykes were pulling into the yard. Sarah waved to Pam. Another wagon followed them down the road.

"Glad to see you," said Mr. Barnes, helping Mrs. Van Dyke step down from the wagon. "Good day, friend," said Mr. Barnes, shaking Mr. Van Dyke's hand. He looked at the wagon coming toward them. "You brought someone with you?" he asked.

Mr. Van Dyke smiled. "Yes. We had a surprise visitor late last night. I think that it is someone you will want to see."

Pam hopped out of the wagon and ran to Sarah. "Hi!" she bubbled. "You'll never guess who it is!"

Sarah studied the wagon carefully as it pulled into the yard. A man rode alone, the reins in his hand. Sarah still couldn't see who it was. Then she heard it. She heard his deep, rich voice, singing out loud and clear. She looked at Pam in disbelief. "It's not …"

"It is," Pam burst out. "It's Pastor Robinson!"

Tears of joy gathered in Sarah's eyes. She had not seen Pastor Robinson for more than a year, not since he had left their little Methodist church to go out and tell the world about the soon return of Jesus Christ.

"Take the baby," said Sarah, handing Samuel to Pam. Pam took Samuel into her arms.

Sarah ran toward the wagon. Tears streamed down her face. "Pastor Robinson!" she called.

Pastor Robinson pulled the wagon to a stop. He jumped out. "Sarah! I almost didn't recognize you. You look so grown up!"

Sarah blushed, and she curtsied politely. Pastor Robinson bowed. Sarah was so happy. She loved Pastor Robinson and had missed him terribly. He hadn't changed a bit.

Mr. Barnes shook Pastor Robinson's hand. "God bless you," Sarah's father said. "Where is your good wife?"

"She stayed behind in Boston with her mother. I had planned on being back there in time for today, but my travels took longer than I had expected. She will forgive me, I'm sure. We will soon be reunited in joy." Pastor Robinson looked expectantly up into the sky.

"Peter will be along shortly," Mr. Van Dyke explained. "He stopped to pick up a friend."

"Is it David Cooper?" Sarah whispered to Pam.

"Yes," Pam nodded. "Mr. Cooper refused to let him leave the house the last few days. Peter went to go and help him sneak out of the house. I hope that they don't get caught."

"Me too," said Sarah.

Sarah's heart pounded. She still couldn't believe that Pastor Robinson was there, and now she was worried about Peter and David.

"Please come inside," said Mr. Barnes. "We have much to celebrate."

Inside, the families gathered around the Barnes's hearth. Pastor Robinson admired baby Samuel and bounced Emily on his knee. He shared many exciting stories about his travels over the past year. They sang hymns and prayed. It was a happy time. They waited joyfully for Jesus' return. All the while, Sarah and Pam exchanged worried looks. They looked out of the window and down the road. Still no Peter or David.

"Sarah," Mrs. Barnes asked, "will you play something for us on your violin, please?"

# SARAH'S DISAPPOINTMENT

Sarah looked around the room. Each person was smiling at her. She didn't really want to play, but she couldn't think of a good reason not to. "Yes, Ma'am," she answered. She climbed the stairs and came back down again, violin in hand. She placed it gently under her chin and tightened each of the strings. "I'll play a piece for you that was my grandfather's favorite," she said, smiling at Grammy. "I look forward to being reunited with him."

Grammy smiled and reached for her handkerchief. She patted her cheeks with it.

Sarah placed the bow on the strings. Music filled the air. *Dear Jesus,* she prayed, as she gently pulled the bow across the strings. *Please come quickly. We are ready for You.*

*Crash! Bang!* The heavy wooden door flew open, and Peter and David stumbled through it. Sarah jumped, and the music came to an end.

# October 22, 1844

Peter looked up, embarrassed. "Sorry to crash in," he said.

"You are forgiven," Mrs. Barnes said and smiled. "Welcome."

"Hello, Mrs. Barnes," Peter and David said together. They bowed.

Pastor Robinson stood and shook David's hand. "I'm proud of you, young man," he said. "How does your family feel about your belief in the Advent Near?"

David pushed his glasses up. Shyly he looked down at the floor. "They don't think highly of it at all, sir," he answered.

Pastor Robinson patted him on the back. "God bless you for your faith," he said.

David's cheeks became red, and he shuffled back to where Peter stood. Quietly, they slipped into the kitchen. Sarah and Pam followed them.

"Can we have a drink of water, Sarah?" Peter asked, wiping his forehead.

"Sure," Sarah replied. She pointed to the

bucket and ladle. Peter and David each took a long drink.

"Now tell us what happened," said Pam.

"It was wild," Peter said, his blue eyes dancing. "Mr. Cooper caught us just as we were climbing out of David's bedroom window."

"Then what happened?" Sarah asked.

"My father told me that I couldn't go with Peter," David answered. His voice shook. "I told him I was going. We had a big fight. He said that I am no longer his son unless I renounce my faith."

"Oh, no," Sarah said. "Peter, when are you going to tell your parents?"

"I hope we won't have to," Peter said. "It will all be over today."

\* \* \* \* \*

A heavy blanket of darkness fell over the Barnes household. Sarah and Pam sat

huddled together on a corner of the sofa.
Sarah tucked her knees up under her chin.
Katie was curled up in a ball at the other
end. She was fast asleep.

Sarah rubbed her eyes. "I'm tired," she
whispered to Pam.

"So am I," Pam said and yawned. "I'm
hungry too."

"Don't even mention being hungry,"
Sarah groaned. "I haven't eaten in two
days!"

"Do you think that Jesus is still coming
today?" Pam whispered.

"I don't know," said Sarah thoughtfully.
"I really don't know."

Mrs. Barnes stood up from her chair
by the fire. She lit a lantern and carried it
over to the dining table, where Mr.
Barnes, Mr. Van Dyke, and Pastor
Robinson sat, studying their Bibles. The
light spread across the pages. "Thank
you," Mr. Barnes whispered.

Mrs. Barnes lifted Emily off the floor.

# SARAH'S DISAPPOINTMENT

Her golden ringlets draped over her mother's arm as she slept. Mrs. Barnes held her close and pulled a blanket over them. Mrs. Van Dyke set Samuel down in the cradle next to Mrs. Barnes. "He's asleep too," she whispered.

David sat in the big chair across from Sarah. He held his Bible up to his nose. He clung to its edges tightly as he read. Peter was stretched out on the floor in front of him, his hands under his head.

Sarah blinked. Her eyelids became heavier and heavier. She struggled to stay awake, but she was very tired. Her eyes closed, and in spite of her best efforts, she began to dream.

Sarah woke up suddenly and rubbed her eyes. She was confused for a moment, and then she remembered where she was. She sat up very carefully, so that she wouldn't wake Pam. The room was still. The men were gone from the dining table.

# October 22, 1844

Everyone else seemed to be asleep. A soft orange glow filled the air.

A movement caught Sarah's eye. David was sitting, his legs curled up against his chest. Noiselessly he sobbed into his hands. The tears streamed past his fingers and ran down his arms. Sarah swallowed hard. She looked out the window. The sun had risen above the horizon. Midnight had passed. Jesus hadn't come. Sarah felt very disappointed.

CHAPTER 6

# A Christmas of Hope

"You're still on this earth, are you, Millerite?"

Sarah frowned and set the hair ribbon she had been holding down on the shopkeeper's shelf. "Merry Christmas to you, too, Nickie," she said, turning around. Nickie's piercing blue eyes met hers.

Nickie shifted her packages from her left hand to her right. "I would have thought that you would have 'gone up' by now," she said, her nose in the air. "Yet, here you are, Christmas shopping just like the rest of us."

Sarah scrunched her eyebrows together. She started to speak, but she was interrupted before she could say anything.

"Leave her alone, Nickie," David said, walking up behind her. His face was nearly buried under a big winter hat.

Nickie spun around angrily and faced her brother. "You're not allowed to talk to her or any other of the 'Millerites'," she snapped.

David clenched his teeth together. "I know what I am allowed and not allowed to do. You are my little sister, and you will listen to me for a change. Leave my friend alone."

Sarah was speechless. She had never heard David speak to Nickie that way before.

Nickie gasped. She swung her ringlets past the fur collar on her cape and over her shoulder. She looked defiantly at David and then at Sarah. "Mother! Father!" she hollered in a shrill voice.

The shopkeeper looked up, annoyed.

Nickie marched across the shop looking for Mr. and Mrs. Cooper.

"You're going to get into trouble," Sarah whispered.

"I know," David said. "The last two months have been miserable. My father won't let me forget that I was wrong, that Jesus didn't come back."

Sarah reached out and touched his hand. David blushed, and Sarah immediately pulled her hand away. *Whoops*, she thought. "Keep your faith," she whispered. "There must be a meaning and a purpose to all of this. God wouldn't abandon us. The Bible is so clear."

David looked over his shoulder. "I know that is true," he whispered hurriedly. "Pray for me. It is so difficult now."

"David Cooper! You step away from that dreadful girl right now!" Mrs. Cooper marched up behind David, her hands on her hips. Her eyes were little slits.

Sarah stepped backward.

Mr. Cooper pushed past his wife and grabbed David by the collar. His moustache twitched, and his face was flushed with anger. "You're coming with me, young man. This will be a very unpleasant Christmas for you."

"What is all of the noise?" Mrs. Barnes walked up the aisle and stood protectively beside Sarah. She carried Samuel in one arm and pulled Emily along by the hand. Katie ran behind her and hid in her skirts.

"It's nothing, Mother," said Sarah quickly. She didn't want to get David into any more trouble.

Mrs. Cooper glared at Mrs. Barnes. "You stay away from our son," she demanded.

# A Christmas of Hope

Mrs. Barnes smiled sympathetically at David. "We will not speak to your son unless he first speaks to us," she said. "Good day, Mrs. Cooper."

Mrs. Barnes turned Sarah around and pulled her out of the shop and onto the busy street. Sarah looked over her shoulder and through the shop window. Mr. Cooper was waving his finger back and forth in front of David's face. Sarah felt sick to her stomach.

Mrs. Barnes almost dragged Sarah down the street and around the corner. Once they were out of sight of the shop, she stopped. "Are you all right, Sarah?" she asked. Her breath made a cloud in the cold air.

"Yes," said Sarah, shaking. "I feel sorry for David."

Mrs. Barnes kissed her forehead. "I know, love," she said. "He is full of faith. God will see him through this."

Sarah smiled. "Thank you, Mother. I hope that you are right."

# SARAH'S DISAPPOINTMENT

"Now, let's keep walking," said Mrs. Barnes. "Your father's meeting should be done by now, and I have a hundred and one things to do before Christmas morning!"

Sarah hurried after her mother. Snowflakes floated through the sky and landed on her nose. She heard bells jingling and carolers sing "Silent Night." The smells and sounds of Christmas were everywhere in Market Square. Mrs. Barnes turned the corner and pulled open the heavy door that led into a large brick building. She held the door open while Emily, Katie, and Sarah walked through it. They stood inside the entranceway, rubbing their arms to keep warm. A group of gentlemen walked through a set of oak doors toward them.

"I see Father," Katie said, pointing at them.

"Just be patient," said Mrs. Barnes. "He'll see us in a minute." She unwrapped

Samuel a little so that he could breathe in some of the warm air.

Mr. Barnes and some of the other men stood talking for a few minutes. Mr. Barnes said goodbye to the others and walked toward his family.

"You all look as if you're frozen," Mr. Barnes said, playfully pinching Emily's nose. Emily giggled.

"How was your meeting?" Mrs. Barnes asked.

"It went well," said Mr. Barnes. "Our committee worked hard the last few months. Now every family in this area will have enough food and clothing for the winter. With so many crops left standing in the fields this fall, it was difficult. We managed to find enough blankets and warm clothes for those who gave away all of their belongings." Mr. Barnes buttoned up his suit coat and pulled on his hat. "Everything is going to be fine. Are you ready to brave that winter wind again?"

Mrs. Barnes pulled a blanket loosely over Samuel's delicate little face. "Let's go," she said.

Sarah followed her mother and father through the busy streets toward the wagon. Emily held on tightly to her hand.

"What do you think I'll get for Christmas, Sarah?" Emily asked as she bounced along beside her.

Sarah laughed. "I don't know, Emily. You'll have to wait and see."

\* \* \* \* \*

The music from the grand piano floated softly through the air. The excitement of Christmas morning had passed, and now Sarah and her family gathered with friends in the Van Dykes' home.

"Have I told you yet how beautiful your dress is?" Pam asked, giggling.

Sarah smoothed her skirt. "Only about a hundred times," she said, laughing.

"Well, it really is," said Pam.

"Thank you," Sarah replied. She had finally finished her dress the week before. It had been very difficult, and she had cried many tears of frustration, but it was done. The broad flat collar sat perched upon the puffy sleeves. It had turned out just as Sarah had dreamed it would.

"Your slippers are lovely too," said Pam.

Sarah pointed her toe admiringly. "Grammy gave them to me this morning for Christmas," she said. "She said that it was time I started dressing like a proper young lady, instead of stomping around like a child!"

Pam giggled. "That sounds just like your Grammy!"

Sarah and Pam walked through the parlor, arm in arm. Sarah nibbled on a piece of orange. A sweet, juicy orange was her favorite Christmas treat.

"School will be starting again in a few weeks," Pam said.

"I know," Sarah answered. "It will be nice to see Alannah more. I've hardly seen her at all the last few weeks. I miss her."

"Me too," said Pam.

Mrs. Van Dyke hurried past them with a tray of mugs full of hot apple cider.

Sarah and Pam walked past Katie, who sat curled up in a red velvet chair by the fire. She was rocking Samuel back and forth in her arms. "Sarah," she whispered loudly, spotting her sister. "Will you take Samuel? I just got him to sleep and now my arms are aching."

"Shh," said Sarah, reaching down and scooping her baby brother out of her sister's arms. "If you just got him to sleep then whisper more quietly."

"Fine," Katie said. She quickly bounced out of the chair and over to the dining table. She helped herself to several cookies and scampered off.

Sarah smiled down at Samuel. "Let's sit for a while," she said to Pam.

"Fine," said Pam. "I'll go and get us a snack."

Sarah sat down in the red velvet chair that Katie had been sitting in. She smiled. Pastor Robinson and her father stood just in front of her. They were deep in conversation. Mr. Barnes and some of the other men were trying to convince Pastor Robinson to stay in Portsmouth. Sarah thought that it might work. Mrs. Robinson had traveled up from Boston to join him. That was a good sign.

"So what you are saying then, Pastor Robinson," Sarah overheard her father say, "is that the cleansing of the sanctuary at the end of the 2,300 days that we thought would be Jesus' return may actually be something else."

"Yes, Edward," Pastor Robinson answered excitedly. "We have always thought that the sanctuary is the earth. What if it isn't the earth? What if it is the sanctuary in heaven?"

"Could there really be a physical sanctuary in heaven?" Mr. Barnes asked.

"I believe the one Moses was instructed to build was a model of something real in heaven," said Pastor Robinson.

Sarah watched her father's face. It was full of wonder. "This would mean that we were wrong about the *event* to occur on October 22, and not the *day*," Mr. Barnes said thoughtfully. "I will need some time to study this for myself, Pastor Robinson. Thank you for sharing it with me."

Mr. Barnes clasped Pastor Robinson's hand.

"Please, study and meditate on it this week," Pastor Robinson said. "There may be a beauty in this disappointment still. I am not alone in coming to these conclusions. Many others have too. Please pray for God's leading to His truth."

"Do you want shortbread or chocolate?"

# A Christmas of Hope

Sarah didn't hear the question. She was thinking about the conversation she had just overheard.

"Sarah, do you want shortbread or chocolate?" Pam held two cookies in front of her.

"Whichever you don't choose is fine with me," Sarah answered, barely paying attention to her best friend. She was still thinking about what Pastor Robinson had said. She didn't understand the details, but there was one important thing that she did understand. She understood that maybe their studies and preparations of the last several years were not all a waste of time. Sarah was overcome with love for her God.

Sarah munched on her shortbread cookie. *I'm sorry if I ever doubted You, God,* she prayed in the quietness of her heart. *Please forgive me.* Sarah felt a peace and assurance that she hadn't felt in months.

"Dear friends and family," said Mr. Van Dyke, standing to get everyone's attention. The music stopped, and the chattering quieted.

"On behalf of my wife and family, I would like to thank you for sharing our home this Christmas day. Before our season of prayer, Peter will share a passage of Scripture with us." Mr. Van Dyke nodded toward his son.

Peter stood in front of his chair. He bent his blond head over his Bible. "I'm reading Hebrews chapter 10, verses 35 to 37," he said. " 'Cast not away therefore your confidence, which hath great recompense of reward. For ye have need of patience, that, after ye have done the will of God, ye might receive the promise. For yet a little while, and he that shall come will come, and will not tarry.' "

Peter closed his Bible and slipped back into his seat.

Sarah thought about the verse Peter had just read. *Perhaps Jesus has a special plan for our lives,* she thought. *He must have a reason for not coming back now.*

Samuel squirmed in her arms and opened his eyes. He looked into his sister's loving face and cooed.

Sarah stroked his soft cheek. "Maybe God has a special plan for you, Samuel," she whispered. "After all, there is no limit to what God can do."

Samuel smiled. She was sure that she was right.

# Get the whole Adventist Girl Series!

These stories about a young pioneer girl named Sarah Barnes take children back in time to the days of William Miller between 1842 and 1844. Even as Sarah's family accepts the message of Jesus' soon return, Sarah must keep up with her daily chores and schoolwork. This four-book historical series will entertain and educate children about the Adventist heritage and hope. 0-8163-1907-3, US$24.99, Cdn$38.99.

Book 1. **A Song for Grandfather.**
Eight-year-old Sarah Barnes can't wait to see Grammy and especially Grandfather! She knows he'll tell her wonderful stories of his life as a sea captain. But Grandpa surprises the whole family with some startling ideas he heard William Miller preach from the Bible. *Jesus will return very soon and the world will come to an end!* Will they accept the message? Paper, 96 pages. 0-8163-1873-5.

Book 2. **Miss Button and the Schoolboard.**
Sarah and her best friend Pam love school—except for those annoying boys and that mean girl Nickie Cooper! Their beloved teacher, Miss Button, is the best teacher in the world. Even so, it's getting harder to be a Millerite and the teasing gets worse. Paper, 96 pages. 0-8163-1874-3.

Book 3. **A Secret in the Family.**
As the Barnes family looks eagerly for the return of Jesus on March 21, 1844, Ma and Pa surprise Sarah with an unexpected announcement: Ma's going to have a baby! Sarah's happy, yet confused. If the world is coming to an end, how does a baby fit into the plan? Paper, 96 pages. 0-8163-1887-5.

Book 4. **Sarah's Disappointment.**
Paper, 96 pages. 0-8163-1888-3.

Order from your ABC by calling **1-800-765-6955**, or get online and shop our virtual store at **www.adventistbookcenter.com**.
- Read a chapter from your favorite book
- Order online
- Sign up for email notices on new products